GOLDCREST FILMS presents
A SULLIVAN BLUTH STUDIOS IRELAND LTD. production

A DON BLUTH FILM

"ROCK-A-DOODLE"

Featuring the voices of GLEN CAMPBELL, EDDIE DEEZEN,
SANDY DUNCAN, ELLEN GREENE, PHIL HARRIS,
CHRISTOPHER PLUMMER, CHARLES NELSON REILLY
and introducing TOBY SCOTT GANGER as Edmond

Songs written by
T.J. KUENSTER
Screenplay by
DAVID N. WEISS
Executive Producers
JOHN QUESTED
MORRIS F. SULLIVAN
Co-Directors
GARY GOLDMAN
DAN KUENSTER
Produced by
DON BLUTH, GARY GOLDMAN, JOHN POMEROY
Directed by
DON BLUTH
Novelization Adapted by
CHIP LOVITT

PROLOGUE

Once upon a time, not so very long ago, the sun came up. Now I know that an everyday sunrise might not seem like a big deal to some folks, but imagine for a moment that instead of rising up, one morning, where *you* lived, the sun took a look around and decided to go back to sleep. It happened to us once.

—*Patou the dog*

CHAPTER 1

It was a farm like any other in the heartland, except for one thing—a rooster named Chanticleer. Chanticleer was no ordinary rooster. His voice was so powerful and his song so sweet that when he sang, the sun came up. All the animals on the farm had jobs to do, and Chanticleer's was to wake up the sun each morning. When he crowed, up came the sun.

Chanticleer had a big heart too, and when he sang, there was plenty of peace and harmony on the farm, and lots of sunshine. Chanticleer was a born crowd-pleaser, and there was no doubt about it, he sure kept all the animals up and shining.

Edmond, a seven-year-old boy, pictured the scene as he listened to his mother, Dory, read him the story of Chanticleer. She sat on his bed reading from an old but beautifully illustrated storybook. Outside Edmond's window, torrents of rain poured down and lightning and thunder shook the sky. Inside Edmond's bedroom, however, it was safe and warm. Edmond's mother's voice was soft and reassuring, and she continued to read her son a bedtime story.

Gazing at the picture of Chanticleer, Edmond could almost hear his song. It was like an invitation, an irresistible invitation not only to the rising sun, but also a call to the other farm animals to arise and begin a new day. He was a handsome bird and all the animals loved to hear him sing. "He sings like a dream," one hen said. "He is a dream," another one sighed. Chanticleer was a rockin' rooster and his voice was truly something special. It had the down–home feel of country morning, but it could rock with the rhythms and energy of the city, which lay beyond the horizon like a jewel a hundred miles to the north. The city pulled some country folk like a magnet and it pulsed to a faster beat than the pleasant life on the farm. Somehow Chanticleer could hear that faraway rhythm, and his song—like the sun—could drive away the rain clouds and brighten the day.

"One morning," continued Edmond's mother, "everything changed. A stranger crept into the barnyard in the pre-dawn darkness, even before Chanticleer woke up. The stranger, a bully of a bird, woke Chanticleer and picked a fight with him. Chanticleer was never one to run away from a fight, and a fierce battle began. Wings flapping, feathers flying, the two roosters wrestled and rolled on the ground and twisted and turned as they fought in midair. In the end, Chanticleer won the fight, but what he didn't know was that the stranger had been sent by the Grand Duke of Owls, a nasty bird. The Duke's bully had done the dirty deed he had been ordered to do. The Duke's plan had succeeded. While the two birds battled, the sun came up over the horizon. Because of the commotion, Chanticleer had forgotten to crow and greet the dawn. The sun had come up without him, and Chanticleer was heartbroken. He thought that perhaps his voice had never raised the sun at all.

"At first the other animals whispered amongst themselves. Then the talk grew louder. An old duck said, 'It came up without him.' 'He's a phony,' another animal shouted. 'You're a fake,' a pig cried. The Duke had turned all the animals against Chanticleer, their best friend. Without a reason to crow anymore, Chanticleer left the farm to find work in the city."

"Mom," Edmond said, "how come the Duke didn't want Chanticleer bringing up the sun?"

"The Duke, like most owls, liked the darkness and the rain," his mother answered.

"I'm not afraid of the dark," Edmond said softly.

Just then there was a crack of thunder and a burst of lightning. The door to Edmond's bedroom burst open and a tall hooded figure stood in the doorway. The hall light behind him cast a dark shadow, and in the dim light, Edmond couldn't see who it was. The figure moved towards his bed.

"You scared me," Dory said. It was her husband Frank.

"Sorry," Frank replied. "We've got big problems out there. If the rain doesn't stop soon, we'll all go floating down the river."

"How bad is it?" Dory asked.

"The river is rising fast. We've got to get all the animals into the barn and reinforce all the sandbags," Frank replied.

"Do you think that will work?" Dory asked worriedly.

"We'll make it work. I'll need some help from the boys," Frank said as he turned and headed down the hall. Edmond heard his father shouting the names of his older brothers, Scott and Mark.

Edmond tore off his blankets and ran to get his clothes. "Me too," he exclaimed.

"Stop right there," his mother ordered.

"Oh, Mom, I'm one of the boys," Edmond protested.

"He meant the big boys," she told him.

"I *am* a big boy," Edmond insisted.

"Not yet you're not, honey," his mother said softly.

"But what can I do?" Edmond asked.

"You can pray for the rain to stop. That will help," she answered.

Down the hall, Scott and Mark were busy trying to find a weather forecast on their radio. When they did they heard the announcer say that the Weather Service was expecting another night of disastrous downpours. A week of rain in the farm belt had caused widespread flooding and the governor was expected to declare a state of emergency if the rains didn't stop soon.

At that moment, their father ran into their room. "Scott and Mark, I need some help getting the animals into the barn. Meet me outside." The boys grabbed their raincoats and heavy boots and ran down the stairs behind their father.

Back in his room, Edmond's mother tucked him in and gave him a kiss. "You stay right here where it's safe, pumpkin. I've got to go and help your father."

After she left, Edmond muttered, "I am too one of the big boys." He picked up the storybook and began to read again.

"Without a reason to crow anymore, Chanticleer left the farm to find work in the city," Edmond said. "Then the rains came . . ."

There was another crack of thunder and the lights suddenly went out. Edmond grabbed his flashlight and ran to the window, still clutching the storybook. He peered out of his window and in the darkness he could see his father and mother struggling to free a large cow that had sunk into knee-deep mud. Frank tied a rope around the cow's middle and then tied the other end to a hitch on their pickup truck. Edmond's mother climbed into the truck and stepped on the accelerator. The tires slipped and skidded in the mud, but finally got enough traction to free the cow.

Edmond laid his book on the windowsill and shined the flashlight on the open pages. He saw a picture of the Grand Duke and poked at the glass monocle in the Duke's eye. "The Duke is causing this storm. I just know it!" he cried. Then he exclaimed, "I know the answer. We need Chanticleer!"

Edmond heard his father yelling outside. "The levee is breaking!" Frank shouted. Edmond could see the water from the flooded river surge over and through the wall of sandbags.

"Frank!" Edmond's mother screamed fearfully.

Edmond opened his window and stuck his head out. The rain drenched his face. "Chanticleer," he screamed into the night. "Chanticleer!"

As he spoke Chanticleer's name, a bolt of lightning struck a large branch of the tree next to Edmond's window. The branch cracked and began to break, and as it did, a powerful gust of wind pushed it against the window. Edmond could hear the sound of the window frame splintering and suddenly the whole room seemed to explode. Edmond closed his eyes and felt the force of the storm wash over him. He felt something hit him in the head, and suddenly stars swirled around him and he seemed to be floating in a sea of debris. Then everything became dark and silent.

CHAPTER 2

When Edmond opened his eyes, he felt a strange presence in the room with him. He heard footsteps, strange footsteps that sounded like claws on a wooden floor.

"Chanticleer?" Edmond called out.

"No," a deep, evil-sounding voice said. "It's not Chanticleer."

"Who are you?" Edmond asked.

"You put your finger in the Duke's face. Don't you remember?"

There was an eerie glow in the room and suddenly Edmond could see a giant owl standing before him. It was the Grand Duke! Edmond had no idea how the Duke had gotten in his room, but there he was. The Duke picked his broken monocle from his eye. "Do you know how expensive these are to replace?" He then threw the monocle on the ground, smashing it to pieces.

The Duke stared menacingly at Edmond and said, "But that is not why the Duke is going to eat you."

"Eat me?" Edmond gulped.

"Oh dear," the Duke said sarcastically. "Now I've gone and spoiled the surprise. Let me explain. We creatures of the night have worked very hard to be absolutely sure that bird does not return. You, with no regard for the feelings of others, have the nerve to call him back here by name. And for what?" the owl asked with a scowl. "So he can spoil this wonderful stormy darkness with his insidious crowing. And besides, I positively loathe that bird's rock 'n' roll," the Duke declared.

Edmond jumped up and ran towards the door. "You're not going to eat me," he said.

The Duke swooped across the room and blocked his path.

"Mom! Dad! Pinch me, I'm dreaming," Edmond cried out. The Duke crept closer but Edmond dodged him and ran towards the other end of his room. The Duke chased Edmond around the room, but couldn't catch him. The Duke was growing frustrated and was breathing heavily.

"I'm getting too old for this," the Duke gasped. "Little boys are so difficult to eat. Kittens are so much more digestible." The Duke drew himself up, took a deep breath, and blew a gust of air towards Edmond. Suddenly, a swirling, glowing cloud surrounded the boy. Edmond struggled against its force, but it was too powerful. Then Edmond's body seemed to disappear. All that was left was a crumpled pair of pajamas.

11

When the cloud lifted, a small furry little kitten peeked its head out of the pajama top. The Duke grabbed it and held it up to its beak to eat it.

"No! No! No!" Edmond screamed. "Mom! Dad! Somebody help me."

But before the Duke could devour Edmond, a large, fierce-looking dog came out of nowhere and bit the Duke on the leg.

"Owww," the Duke screamed. He tried to shake it off, but the dog wouldn't let go. The Duke dropped the kitten, which ran and hid in the corner. The dog and the Duke continued to fight a fierce battle.

"Patou, you'll pay for this," the Duke threatened. "This does not concern you."

The dog replied, "It does if it's about Chanti."

The kitten saw a flashlight nearby and remembered that owls hate the light. The flashlight was twice his size, but he somehow managed to turn it on. He aimed the light at the Duke and the owl recoiled in horror. The Duke let go of Patou and flew frantically back into the night.

When Patou caught his breath, he turned to the kitten and said, "That flashlight business was mighty quick thinking. My name is Patou. What's your name, little fella?"

"Edmond," the kitten replied nervously. "Is he gone?"

"Yeah, he's gone, but he'll be back, and he

won't be back alone, that coward. I would have whopped him good if I'd had my shoes tied. Tying shoes is tougher than dried dog food."

"What is a dog doing wearing shoes?" asked Edmond.

"I got a load of bunions and these shoes help my feet," Patou explained.

"Let me show you how to tie them," the kitten volunteered. But when Edmond reached out to tie the shoes, he saw his hands had become paws.

"Jeepers! I'm all furry!" he screamed.

"Well," said Patou matter-of-factly, "kittens are furry."

"But . . . but . . . I'm a little boy!" Edmond cried. Suddenly a loud meow rose out of Edmond's throat. "Did that come out of me?" he asked. Then he saw his image in the mirror.

"I'm a cat," he shrieked. "The Duke turned me into a cat! I can't be a cat. I'm a boy! What will I do, Patou?"

"Steady, boy," Patou said calmly. "Keep your pants on."

Edmond looked down and blushed. He wasn't wearing any pants. He grabbed the shirt from a nearby frontiersman doll and pulled it on. It reached all the way to his knees. On the floor next to him was the doll's coonskin cap. He picked it up and plunked it on his head.

Edmond was still reeling from the shock of being

turned into a cat when he heard a voice coming from outside. It was a high voice, one with a slight lisp.

"This can't possibly be the city," said the voice. Out of the rain and in through Edmond's window came a small bespectacled mouse wearing a yellow slicker and clutching a map. Edmond felt a strange sensation come over him. He suddenly leapt at the mouse, claws ready. The frightened mouse ran away and back out the window.

"It's okay, Peepers," Patou called to the mouse. "It's only Edmond. He won't hurt you. He's a nice little kitty."

"I'm a boy," Edmond cried. "And I almost ate a mouse. I must be crazy," he said disgustedly.

"You bet your sweet whiskers," Peepers replied as she marched back into the room. Following right behind Peepers was a parade of other barnyard animals. There were pigs, baby chicks, horses, and other animals.

"There ain't no city here," a turkey said.

"Oh sadness," said a pig named Stuey.

Patou turned back to Edmond. "Hey! Aren't you going to help me tie my shoes?"

"I can't help anybody. I'm small. I'm too little. I'm a scrawny little furball runt," Edmond said sadly. "Mom and Dad won't even recognize me."

Edmond walked over to his window and yelled, "Mom! Dad!" but there was no reply.

Just then a bolt of lightning lit the sky and thunder boomed. All the animals huddled together.

"Oh, Chanticleer," Edmond sighed.

"What did you say?" Patou said.

"If Chanticleer doesn't come back and crow, the sun won't ever shine and the rain will keep coming down," Edmond explained. "The water will get higher and higher till . . . till . . . we all drown."

Edmond heard wings fluttering and saw a big black bird fly into the room. It was a magpie named Snipes, another of the barnyard animals. He surveyed the scene.

"Wowee, wowee, wowee! Are we near the city yet? We magpies were made for the city," Snipes exclaimed wildly.

"We're not looking for the city, Snipes," said Peepers. "We're looking for Chanticleer."

"Well, he is in the city, isn't he?" Snipes pointed out.

"Chanticleer in the city?" Edmond asked. "Then it's true," he said. "You laughed at him and he went away."

"You're right, son," Patou said softly. "We done wrong. That's why we're searching for the city, to find Chanti and apologize."

"So he'll forgive us and come home and raise the sun," a chorus of baby chicks said plaintively.

"I know where the city is," Edmond declared. "I've been there lots of times as a boy."

"As a boy?" Snipes said skeptically.

"Yes. I was a boy before that big owl turned me into a cat," Edmond explained angrily.

"An owl?" Stuey the pig snorted nervously.

"Will you take us to the city?" Peepers asked.

"I can't," Edmond said dejectedly. "Look at me. I'm a cat. . . . No, I'm a little kitty. What can I do?"

"Lots of things," Peepers said. "I can do lots of things and I'm a lot smaller than you. Furthermore, I can also forgive you for being a cat . . . if you take us to the city. That is, unless you're a 'fraidy cat?"

"I am not afraid," Edmond replied.

"A scaredy cat?" Peepers suggested.

"Me, scared? I'm not scared of anything," Edmond answered. "I'll take you to the city and we'll find Chanticleer and bring him home and save Mom and Dad, and the farm, too." All the animals cheered.

"Let's go," Edmond shouted, leaping on Patou's back.

"Hey, guys," Snipes called out. He was sitting high above them on a half-demolished wall. "Hope you can swim."

Suddenly a wall of water flooded the room. The animals scurried to safety, climbing on a table and other pieces of furniture that floated by.

"We don't have to swim," Edmond said. "We'll go by boat." Edmond and Patou jumped into Edmond's toy box, which was now floating in the water. Snipes joined them a minute later.

Peepers had scrambled to safety on a bed which was floating in the water. Patou tossed her the flashlight and some batteries. "You'll need this in case the owls return," he advised.

"Owls?" the animals asked anxiously.

"I'm going with you," Peepers declared as she swam over to the toy box and climbed in.

"Good luck with the owls," Edmond called to the remaining animals as the toy box bobbed out the open window.

"To the city!" Snipes exclaimed.

CHAPTER 3

Swirling clouds filled the sky and lightning cracked as the Duke sat at a huge pipe organ in his lair in the woods. Above him flew his army of evil owls.

"So," the Duke continued his story, "the kitty turns on me. And what do you think he turns on the Duke?"

"What, master?" the owls asked.

"A flashlight," he said with a sneer.

"What a horrible thing to do," the owls said with a shudder.

"And while my back was turned," the Duke went on, "what lousy, four-legged, flea-bitten louse comes sneaking in through the window and bites my leg?"

"Who?" asked the owls. "Who-who-who?"

"Patou, that's who!" the Duke said angrily. "Destroy the farm. Destroy the cat and the dog," the Duke ordered. "Or do you want the chicken back?"

"No," they shrieked. "We hate the sun. The answer's no!"

"Besides," the Duke said, "it'll make my leg

feel so much better if that rooster never crows again!''

The owls flew in a frenzied circle, singing:

We hate the sun,
That much we know.
We hate the rooster,
From head to toe.
We hate the sun,
From head to toe.
We hate the rooster.
Never let him crow!

''Never let him crow!'' the Duke repeated with utter fury in his voice. His owls flew off into the darkness.

Just then a sour note sounded on the organ. A small nearsighted owl had crashed down on the keyboard of the pipe organ.

''Uncle Dukey! Uncle Dukey!'' the little owl sputtered. It was the Duke's nephew, Hunch.

''I told you never to call me that,'' the Duke replied icily.

''Yes, sir. I mean no, sir,'' Hunch sputtered. ''Guess what I saw? Patou the dog floating down the river in a toy box and he has this cute little kitty with him.''

''My little . . . I mean, my big nephew. Come to Uncle and tell me about it,'' the Duke said ever so sweetly.

Meanwhile, Edmond and his friends continued to float through the perilous flood waters. The animals had rigged up a lookout post for Edmond, since he was the only one who knew the way to the city.

Edmond recognized an ice-cream stand he and his family had passed on their trips to the city. He announced that they had to make a right turn at the stand.

"Starboard, ho," Peepers ordered.

"Starboard who?" Snipes asked. "Is that left or right?"

"Right," Edmond answered. A few moments later he cried out, "Giant tree floating in the water, 100 feet ahead."

The toy box seemed to be heading right towards it. "90 feet and closing," Edmond shouted. "80 feet, 70 feet, 60 feet," he warned.

"We need wind power," Peepers yelled.

"40 feet . . . 30 feet . . ." Edmond screamed.

"I think I'm slowing you down, guys," Snipes said as he flew into the air and circled a few feet above the toy box.

Patou grabbed a blanket that was in the bottom of the box and rigged up a makeshift sail. A sudden gust of wind caught the sail and Patou, using a tennis racket as a rudder, managed to steer the toy box past the tree.

Patou's ears perked up. "I hear something," he said. It was the sound of flapping wings. A group of owls was flying above them. As usual, Hunch was bringing up the rear.

"You heard the Duke," Hunch said. "Total and complete annihilation. Bombs away!"

The owls swooped down to attack. Patou and Peepers struggled to close the toy box lid, but before they had a chance, the owls were upon them. It was a furious fight and the owls seemed to have the upper hand. However, Peepers saved the day when she found Edmond's camera in the toy box. She grabbed the camera and pointed it at the owls. "Say cheese," she said as she jumped on the shutter button. The camera's built-in flash exploded with a blast of blinding light. The owls screamed in pain and they flew away.

From high overhead Hunch watched the toy box float towards a narrow pipe. As the water approached the pipe, it picked up speed until it was a raging torrent, all heading for one narrow opening. They were doomed, Hunch thought. From his position, he could barely make out the words above the pipe. They read: Danger! Keep Out! and letters that Hunch thought spelled out Adequate Pipe.

"Total and complete annihilation," Hunch said proudly. Hunch flew off to tell the Duke the good news.

Back in his dark lair, the Duke was preparing his dinner, a skunk pie. He was about to put the pie in the oven when Hunch swooped in. As usual, Hunch miscalculated his landing and knocked the pie to the floor, totally ruining the Duke's dinner plans.

The Duke was furious. "If I killed my nephew, would it be murder or charity?" he muttered, an evil edge in his voice.

"I got him," Hunch said excitedly. "I really got him. No more kitty, sir. Mission accomplished."

"And the dog?" asked the Duke.

"Gone. Wiped out. Total and complete annihilation."

"Annihilation? How did you do it?" the Duke demanded.

"Adequately," Hunch replied.

"What is that supposed to mean?" the Duke asked.

"They were sucked down an adequate pipe," Hunch explained. "At least that's what the sign said. Danger. Adequate Pipe."

"Oh, dear," groaned the Duke. "Come to Uncle." The Duke began screaming at his nephew. "You imbecile. It wasn't an adequate pipe. It was an aqueduct pipe. It leads straight to the city."

The Duke seethed with anger. "I'll give you one more chance," he told Hunch. "It's them or you. Get to the city, now!" he ordered.

"Not the city," Hunch said, shaking with fear. "It's too bright. I'll go blind. I may die!"

"Say it isn't so," the Duke said sarcastically as he tossed Hunch a pair of sunglasses. "Now GO!"

As the Duke suspected, Edmond and his friends

had survived the owls' attack, and were now racing down the aqueduct pipe in their makeshift toy box boat. They had managed to slam the lid down just as they were swept into the water-filled pipe.

However, they were far from being out of danger. After the toy box was swept into the aqueduct pipe, Snipes began to act crazily. Although there was plenty of air in the toy box, Snipes felt as if he couldn't breathe.

"I need air," he complained. "We're trapped."

"He's claustrophobic, you know," Peepers explained. "He gets nervous in closed-in spaces."

Suddenly Snipes began pecking holes in the box with his beak. However, instead of air coming in through the holes, water began to pour in. As Snipes pecked more holes, more water came in. Soon, the box was three-quarters full and the animals were trying desperately to keep their heads above the water.

"Hold still, you crazy bird," Patou yelled. He grabbed Snipes and took a paddle and rubber toy that had been in the box. He quickly wrapped the rubber toy around Snipes' beak and then tied him to the paddle. He was immobilized, but the damage had been done. In a few minutes, the box would be completely filled with water. Just when it seemed like it was all over, the box fell out of the pipe and into a large chamber.

Suddenly it was calm again. The animals opened the box and noticed that right in front of them was the end of the chamber. Ahead of them was a huge waterfall.

"Abandon ship," shouted Patou.

Before they had a chance to jump out, however, the box was carried over the edge and down the waterfall. The box hit the bottom and shattered into pieces.

One by one, the animals drifted up to the surface. A passing garbage can floated by and they all jumped on it.

"Look," shouted Edmond as he pointed ahead of them. "The city."

There in front of them lay the city with its tall buildings and what seemed like a million bright lights. It beckoned like a dream.

"It's so beautiful," said Peepers.

"Wow!" said Snipes.

"Now all we have to do is find Chanticleer," Patou commented. "And that's going to be like hunting for a needle in a haystack."

CHAPTER 4

Finally the animals reached the city and dry land. After floating through the flood waters and the aqueduct pipe, it felt good to be able to step on solid ground again. The animals made their way to a restaurant phone booth and they proceeded to look for Chanticleer's name in the phone book. "Let's see," said Edmond as he looked through the listings. "There's Chalmers, Chanta, Chantilly, Chantz, Chapman, but no Chanticleer."

The animals wandered through the streets of the city. They looked everywhere and talked to everyone, but no one had ever heard of Chanticleer. Every place they went, however, they saw posters and bright neon signs that flashed the name of The King. The King was the biggest music star the city had ever seen. The King had recorded dozens of hit songs and he had millions of fans.

After a hard day of searching for Chanticleer, the animals sat down to rest on the curb outside a huge theater called Pinky's Palace. Towering over them was an enormous and elaborate neon sign of

The King himself, strumming a gigantic neon guitar with a neon hand that moved up and down.

"You know," said Patou, "somehow I get the feeling that Chanticleer is right under our noses."

The King himself was performing that very night at Pinky's Palace, but the animals were in no mood for music. They were tired, and Patou's feet hurt. And, as usual, his shoes were untied.

"For the hundredth time, Patou," Edmond said as he helped the dog tie his shoes, "it's over, around, under, and through. That's how Patou ties his shoe. Now you say it."

Circling high above the theater was a small owl wearing sunglasses. It was Hunch. In his hand he clutched his all-purpose knife, which contained a can opener, flyswatter, corkscrew, and a dozen other devices. Ready for action, he flicked a switch and out popped an umbrella. "Oops, wrong one," he said with a demented smile. He flicked the switch again and a huge razor-sharp blade popped out.

"Pilot to bombardier," he muttered to himself, "I'm going in for a closer look. Total and complete atrocitation!"

Miscalculating his landing, Hunch crashed through some trees and landed with a thud on the sidewalk. For the time being, he was too stunned to move.

Soon hundreds of excited music fans began arriving at Pinky's Palace for the show. They jammed the sidewalk and streets and marveled at the colorful neon sign of The King.

"This is tiring just sitting here," Peepers complained. "If you ask me . . ."

"We didn't," wisecracked Snipes.

But Peepers didn't hear him. She too was staring intently at the giant neon sign.

"Jumping Jehosephat," she exclaimed. "It's him!"

"Who?" asked Snipes.

"No wonder we couldn't find him. Chanticleer changed his name. He's The King!"

"Chanticleer is The King?" Edmond asked excitedly. Sure enough, when they studied the giant neon sign, it was clear The King was a rockin' rooster, and despite the new hairdo and image, it was clearly Chanticleer.

"Oh, Your Highness," Patou said respectfully.

Just then the animals heard the announcer's voice from inside the theater.

"Ladies and gentlemen, The King!"

Inside the theater, The King appeared onstage wearing a white jumpsuit with spangles that shone like diamonds when the spotlight caught them. And when the rockin' rooster began singing, the fans went wild.

Backstage in his office The King's manager, a large weasel named Colonel Pinky, was counting the money from ticket sales. "That's $111,332, less my fee of 60%," he said excitedly. With him was Goldie Pheasant, a beautiful singer and dancer who longed to be a star, too.

"Colonel Pinky," she pleaded. "I've just got to know when . . ."

"Goldie," interrupted the Colonel. "Must you bother me with this right now? You've got to go on in two minutes."

"But I'm too good for the chorus."

"Everybody starts out in the chorus," the Colonel responded.

Goldie heard the crowd applauding for The King and was jealous. She asked, "What's he got that I haven't got?"

"A voice," replied the Colonel. "Look here, Goldie. When I found The King, nobody wanted him. Nobody cared about him. I picked him up out of the gutter and now look at him. I made him a star. I can do that for you too, Goldie, if you just do as I tell you." Goldie left the room and headed towards the stage.

Thirty minutes later The King was wrapping up his last number. "Thank you," he said to the cheering crowd. "Thank you very much. I love you!" The fans went wild, giving him a standing ovation and chanting, "We want The King."

Back outside the theater, Hunch had recovered. He stood pressed against the theater wall right next to the doors and was creeping towards the animals with his knife poised when a voice boomed over the loudspeakers.

"The King is leaving the building," the announcer said. And with that, the doors flew open, smashing Hunch into the wall. Dazed, he stumbled out, just as a red carpet was rolled out. The carpet rolled on top of Hunch, trapping him beneath the feet of a dozen burly toad bodyguards.

"Get out of the way," one muscular bodyguard shouted to the crowd.

"Don't touch the star," another yelled.

"Move it!" screamed another.

"We want The King. We want The King," the crowd of fans chanted.

The King dashed out through the crowd and waved to the fans. Edmond screamed out Chanticleer's name but his voice was drowned out by the chanting crowd. Edmond and his friends couldn't get near The King. The star slipped into a huge limousine waiting alongside the curb and sped away.

Hunch crawled out from beneath the carpet, bruised and confused. "Total aggravation," he moaned.

Leaving the limo, The King and the Colonel boarded a helicopter which soared up and away from the cheering throng.

"Whew," exclaimed the Colonel as the helicopter rose through the night sky. "You were fantastic tonight, King. Really."

The King didn't respond to the Colonel's compliments. All the excitement from his concert had worn off. Now The King lay motionless on a huge bed.

"Really great show tonight, King," the Colonel repeated. "What can I get you? A beach house in Maui? If you want, I'll buy the entire island."

"No, thanks, Colonel," The King responded, staring at the ceiling.

"Say, what's eating you?" the Colonel asked.

"Well, I don't know, Colonel. I guess I'm just a little lonely," The King said softly.

"Are you crazy? 20,000 people scream your name and you're lonely?" the Colonel declared. "I love this guy."

"Yeah, but it's not like it was down on the farm," The King said wistfully.

"You told me yourself what they did to you. They don't love you," the Colonel said.

Then he yelled into his portable phone.

"Murray," he screamed. Murray was the copter pilot. "Give us a roll to the right so we can get a better view of the crowd."

The helicopter dipped to the right and the Colonel and The King looked out the window. They could see a huge, heart-shaped crowd below and they could still hear the fans chanting, "We want The King."

"They love you," the Colonel shouted over the sound of the spinning helicopter blades. "You're The King! You were incredible tonight."

"Well, that's nice," The King said. He walked back to the bed, lay down, and said, "Wake me when we get there."

Meanwhile, back at the flooded farmhouse, Stuey the pig and the other animals were growing nervous. They had no idea how much longer the flashlight batteries would last.

"Stuey," one of the bunnies cried out, "they're fading fast."

"Do we have any more batteries?" Stuey asked.

"Only two," the bunny answered.

"Oh sadness," moaned Stuey.

Just then a phone that was sitting on a nearby table rang. Stuey hopped onto a dressmaker's mold and paddled over to the floating table to answer the phone.

"Hello. Who is it? What do you want? We've got our own emergency here. Yeah. Who? Edmond?" Stuey turned to the other animals. "Anyone named Edmond around here?"

"This is Edmond," the voice at the other end of the line shouted. "I'm Edmond, the little boy . . . I mean the little kitty," Edmond said. "We made it to the city."

"Oh," said Stuey, "it *is* the kid."

"Stuey," the bunny screamed. "The flashlight is going out!"

"Our lights are going out," Stuey said to Edmond. "We're running out of time. We need Chanticleer quick."

"We'll be there as soon as we can," Edmond promised.

"Bye, kitty," Stuey said. "Gotta go." Stuey dropped the phone and it fell into the water.

Edmond shouted into the mouthpiece, "Stuey! Stuey! What about my family? Are they all right?"

Edmond could hear the sound of the phone being pulled up through the water. He listened and heard a familiar voice. It was the Duke! He had swooped down and plucked the phone out of the water.

"Hello. It's the Duke," the owl said into the mouthpiece. "I have some rather bad news, I'm afraid." He paused for a moment and cleared his throat. "When the batteries expire, so will your friends. Toodle-oo. Cheerio. Bye," he said and hung up.

"Oh, no!" cried Edmond. Suddenly the phone line went dead.

The Duke and his owls decided to wait on the farmhouse roof. "Tweedleedee, Tweedleedee, they're running out of batteries," they sang.

"Not yet we're not," the bunny shouted as she jammed two fresh ones into the flashlight. She aimed it through the hole in the roof, then turned it on. The blast of light sent the owls scurrying for darkness again.

Chanticleer was a rockin' rooster and his voice was truly something special.

A stranger crept into the barnyard, waking Chanticleer and picking a fight with him.

The Grand Duke sitting at his huge pipe organ with his army of evil owls.

Patou rubber-banded Snipes' beak to stop him from pecking more holes in the toy box.

Edmund, Patou, Snipes and Peepers arriving in the city to find Chanticleer.

Chanticleer's friends are tied to a ceiling fan after being caught by Colonel Pinky.

The hungry owls atop the farmhouse roof waiting for the flashlight to go out.

Chanticleer, Edmund and Patou singing a song on the barnyard fence enjoying a sunny day.

CHAPTER 5

Several nights later, The King was to perform another show at Colonel Pinky's Palace. As the Colonel's limousine made its way towards the Palace, the King awoke from a nap and began strumming his guitar lazily in the backseat. As he did, the Colonel's portable phone rang. The Colonel picked it up.

"Hello," he said. "Who? You say a dog, a cat, a mouse, and a bird, what? What is this, some kind of joke?"

It was the Duke on the other end of the line. He explained why he was calling.

"I don't think it's funny at all. They want to take the rooster back to the farm. Listen, you don't want that. I don't want that. He makes you lots of money. He makes me miserable. Your chicken thinks that they don't want him on the farm. Well, that's good. All you have to do is make sure he keeps thinking that. It wouldn't be too good for either of us if his friends should get a chance to talk to your chicken. Understood?"

"Yeah!" the Colonel exclaimed. "Thanks a million. It's been most enlightening."

Soon the limousine pulled up in front of Pinky's Palace. Neon lights flashed The King's name and giant spotlights crisscrossed the sky. A huge crowd, including Edmond and his friends, gathered in front of the theater. Thanks to the Duke's warning, the Colonel and his bouncers were on the lookout for Edmond and the rest of the animals. A huge banner saying, "No Dogs, Cats, Birds, or Mice Allowed In" was hung in the front of the theater, and huge bouncers stood at the doors ready to enforce the rule.

Of course, The King had many fans who happened to be dogs, cats, birds, and mice, and they all desperately wanted to see the show. The sign hadn't said anything about penguins, so an enterprising character outside the theater was making a small fortune selling penguin suits to those fans barred from entering. Edmond, Patou, Peepers, and Snipes each bought penguin suits and managed to sneak into the show.

Once inside, the group made their way to a table overlooking the stage. While Snipes gorged himself on lasagna, Edmond was busy writing a note. It read:

Dear Chanticleer,
    We're sorry. Please come home.

                            Your friends,

"Here guys, sign this," Edmond said. Patou, Snipes, and Peepers all placed their handprints at the bottom.

Peepers turned to a tough-looking waiter standing near their table. "Would you see that The King gets this letter, please?"

"It's very important," Edmond added.

The waiter read the note and picked up a nearby phone and said, "Get me da boss."

Backstage, the Colonel and Goldie Pheasant were having a little talk. The Colonel wanted Goldie to make sure Edmond and his friends didn't get near The King.

"It sounds bad, Colonel Pinky," Goldie murmured.

"It's only a little itty-bitty bad," the Colonel said. "It's not a big bad. Look, The King's lonely and that bad little kitty wants to steal him away from us. The kitty and his friends want to take The King away. Now you don't want that, do you?"

Goldie didn't answer. She still wasn't happy about her part in the production.

"Just get out there and do the number. Make him happy," the Colonel said, pointing to The King. "Just make sure you keep him away from that kitty."

Just then the Colonel's phone rang and he went into his office to answer it.

Suddenly the announcer's voice boomed out over

the loudspeakers. "Ladies and gentlemen, Pinky's Palace proudly presents . . . The King."

The crowd roared as The King appeared. The set was a giant underwater scene complete with a sunken ship and a half-dozen shark figures circling overhead. From their table, Edmond and his friends could see The King as he sang and strutted across the stage.

"Would you look at that," whispered Patou.

"Is that Chanticleer?" asked an incredulous Peepers.

Four huge bouncers approached the table. Edmond sensed that they hadn't delivered the note, so he quickly scribbled another one and got the animals to put their prints on it again. Obviously the penguin disguises hadn't fooled the bouncers.

"Youse guys are dead meat. We said, 'No Dogs, Cats, Boids, or Meeces Allowed,' " one of the bouncers snarled.

Edmond quickly folded the second letter into a paper airplane and tossed it towards the stage. "Chanticleer," he yelled.

As the bouncers began to chase the animals, the plane sailed down over the heads of the audience toward The King. It almost hit The King's hand, but at the last minute, an air current lifted the note into the air and right into the mouth of one of the shark figures that circled above The King's head.

Pursued by the bouncers, Edmond and his friends shed their penguin suits and grabbed some lobster costumes they found in a costume rack backstage.

As they ran past the Colonel, he took one look at them and knew something fishy was going on.

"Hey, there are no lobsters in this number! Get them out of here," he screamed. The animals split up and ran in different directions. Edmond scrambled up a rope ladder that led to the upper reaches of the stage, followed by one of the Colonel's goons. The revolving sharks were right below him and Edmond jumped onto the one whose mouth held the paper airplane note. The extra weight made the ring of sharks shift to one side. Luck was on Edmond's side and the shark dipped right as it approached The King. As he whirled by, Edmond placed the note into The King's hand. But the King was so engrossed in his song, he didn't really pay attention to what had happened.

The Colonel had seen the note fly into The King's hand and he whispered something to Goldie. "Now," the Colonel ordered, and he pushed Goldie out onto the stage. Goldie danced over to The King and gave him a kiss. The King was so totally distracted by Goldie that he didn't notice that she had plucked the note out of his hand.

Patou, who had escaped his pursuers, saw what had happened. "Oh, no," he moaned. He was beginning to think that they would never be able to get to Chanticleer.

During the next few days, Goldie and The King

spent a lot of time together. Suddenly The King wasn't lonely anymore. The Colonel had told Goldie to pretend she was in love with The King. But the truth of the matter was that she was really falling in love with the singing star. Goldie felt like a different person. Gone was the jealous chorus girl. She could now see that despite The King's fancy costumes and his stardom, he was really a quiet and unpretentious country boy who needed a friend.

Edmond and his friends spent their next few days wandering through the city planning their next move. One morning they passed by a newsstand filled with papers. One headline announced: "Colonel Pinky Signs The King to 6 Movie Deals." Another declared: "Goldie Pheasant to Star in The King's New Picture."

The animals decided their best chance was to try to talk to Goldie at the movie studio where she was filming The King's latest picture. The animals snuck into the studio and Edmond set out to find Goldie's trailer room. When he found it, he hid behind the cans of hairspray and bottles of perfume. Goldie was sitting in front of the mirror putting on her makeup. Edmond stepped out from behind the hairspray cans and said, "Excuse me, ma'am."

Goldie was quite startled.

"You're the only one who can help us," Edmond pleaded. "We have to talk to Chanticleer, I mean The King. You see, there's this terrible flood, and if he doesn't come home and crow . . .''

"Wait a minute," Goldie interrupted. "You're the little kitty Colonel Pinky told me about. You're bad."

"I am not bad," Edmond protested.

"You go away now," Goldie demanded. When Edmond didn't move, she picked up a jar of makeup and tossed it at him. It shattered around him. Then she screamed.

Edmond ran out of the trailer, but thanks to Goldie's screaming, he and his friends were captured. They were taken to the Colonel's trailer where the goons threw a net over them, tied it shut, then hoisted it up in the air and tied it to a ceiling fan.

Goldie was very upset. The Colonel had said that no one would get hurt, but now it appeared as if The King's friends were in serious danger. She suddenly felt ashamed and a tear rolled down her cheek.

As if Edmond and the animals didn't have enough to worry about, Hunch had followed them to the studio and found them in the Colonel's trailer. When he looked through the window and saw Edmond and his friends tied up in the net, he thought they would be easy pickings. "Total and complete annihilation," he predicted.

Hunch cut a hole in the top of the trailer with his knife and tried to sneak in. But he miscalculated again and crashed down onto the trailer floor. Seeing the animals helplessly trapped in the net, he gleefully muttered, "Anticipation."

Hunch flicked his knife and out popped a large, sharp fork. He jumped on a TV set and reared back as he prepared to leap towards the net with the fork aimed at the animals.

"Acceleration," he said with a grin. As he did, he brought the fork back over his head to get as much momentum as possible. However, the fork touched the TV antenna wires, causing an electrical short-circuit. Sparks flew and electricity ran through Hunch's body, zapping him and sending him around the room like a runaway rocket.

The shock caused a second short-circuit in the trailer's electrical system and everything went haywire. The ceiling fan suddenly started spinning swiftly. As it did, the rope holding the net with Edmond and his friends became twisted. It began to fray and a few moments later, it snapped, dropping the animals onto the Colonel's sofa. They quickly freed themselves. Hunch was stunned and staggering, and he was out of commission for a few minutes, but still very much a threat.

Meanwhile, on the movie set, The King and Goldie were filming a scene while sitting on a motorcycle. Goldie was upset and she was having trouble with the scene. So was Murray, who was handling the special effects. Snow began falling on the set as Murray fed pillows into a huge grinder. Feathers suddenly covered the sound-stage.

"Murray," the Colonel yelled. "There's no snow in this scene. It's supposed to be summer. And how about a smile, Miss Pheasant," the Colonel said with exasperation. It was time for a break anyway, so he yelled, "Everybody, take five!"

Goldie whispered in The King's ear, "King, can I talk to you for a minute?"

The King thought Goldie was simply nervous about appearing in her first film, so he said, "Now, Goldie, don't you worry. You're going to do just fine."

Goldie pulled out the paper plane note that Edmond had written. "But, King . . ." she started to say.

"No buts about it, darlin'," The King said, taking the letter and tossing it aside.

"King, I've done something awful," she sobbed.

"What is it, babe?" The King said.

Goldie picked up the note and handed it to The King. "Here, read this," she said, picking up the crumpled note.

The King's eyes narrowed and his brow grew furrowed as he read the note and recognized Patou's, Peepers', and Snipes' handprints.

"Where did you get this?" he asked.

"I took it from you during the show the other night," she answered.

"They were here?" asked the King.

"They're still here," Goldie replied.

"Why didn't you tell me?" The King demanded to know.

"Because she wasn't supposed to," yelled the Colonel who had been eavesdropping nearby. Goldie gasped. "I'm disappointed in you, Goldie. I said to entertain him, not educate him."

"Colonel, what's this all about?" The King said, his voice growing more forceful.

"Don't worry, King. Your friends are fine," Colonel Pinky promised.

"No, they're not," cried Goldie. "They're tied up in his . . ."

"Shut up!" Colonel Pinky shouted.

"Where are they?" The King demanded. He grabbed Colonel Pinky by the shirt collar and began shaking him. But Colonel Pinky was a big and powerful weasel and he tossed The King off easily. The Colonel's goons grabbed him and held him.

"Don't hurt him, boys," the Colonel said calmly. "He's got a movie to make."

"I ain't making nothing with you," The King said defiantly.

"Now, King," the Colonel drawled, "I got a lot of money invested in this thing. I don't want to lose my money.'' He paused and a smile appeared on his lips. ''And you don't want to lose your friends, now do you?''

''That's blackmail!'' The King shouted angrily.

''That's show biz,'' the Colonel countered. ''Makeup!'' he screamed.

CHAPTER 6

Reluctantly, The King and Goldie returned to the movie set and resumed filming the motorcycle scene. This time, however, The King was not about to follow the script as it was written. He had some serious improvising in mind.

"I'm sorry," Goldie whispered.

"Don't talk to me," The King said. "I'm thinking. Where are they?"

"In Colonel Pinky's trailer outside," she answered.

"Stand by. Quiet on the set," a crew member shouted.

"Action," yelled Colonel Pinky.

Action was exactly what The King had in mind. He started the motorcycle engine and rocked the motorcycle off its stand. He tore off the set, pulling a wheelie as he raced out the stage door.

"That's not in the script. Stop them!" the Colonel screamed, sending six gator goons on motorcycles after them.

In Colonel Pinky's trailer Hunch was still trying to attack Edmond and his friends.

"Annihilation. Abomination. Hold still!" he demanded.

Now that they were free the animals easily dodged Hunch's clumsy moves. Patou picked up a frying pan from the kitchen area and swung it at Hunch. But just as he began his swing, The King and Goldie crashed through the door on the motorcycle. The door flew open smashing Hunch against the wall, but Patou was already in mid-swing. He slugged The King in the head, knocking him off the motorcycle and knocking him out.

Patou looked at The King. "I think I killed him," he said fearfully.

"Chanticleer," screamed Edmond.

"He's dead. He's dead. He's dead," wailed Snipes.

Peepers was the only one who wasn't panicking. She calmly walked over to The King and lifted his eyelid. She looked deep into his eye and announced, "He's not dead."

Edmond and his friends heard the roar of motorcycles outside the trailer. They looked out the window and saw a gang of alligator goons racing towards them.

"Let's get him out of here," Patou said, lifting the motionless body of The King onto his back. "Through there," he said pointing to the back window. While the Colonel's goons crept up to the front door, Patou, Edmond, and all the rest of the animals made their escape.

They spotted the Colonel's pink Cadillac and jumped into it.

"Can you drive a car?" Edmond asked Peepers.

"Piece of cake," Peepers replied. "Edmond, you steer."

"Steer? I've never driven a car. We'll crash," Edmond protested.

"Do it! Don't be such a scaredy cat," Peepers ordered.

Peepers turned the key and the engine roared. Snipes gave the gas pedal a push and the Caddy took off with its wheels squealing. Steering was difficult because the Colonel's huge trailer was still attached to the back of the Cadillac. The car raced down the street with the trailer swinging wildly behind it. Close behind were a gang of gator goons on motorcycles and Colonel Pinky and Murray, who were riding in a pink studio cart.

Edmond looked in his side view mirror and saw Hunch inching his way along the side of the trailer using suction cups to prevent him from falling off.

If he could reach the Cadillac, Hunch thought, he would put an end to this adventure once and for all. "Complete abomination," he said, clutching his knife.

The car was picking up speed. Edmond was terrified.

"Open your eyes, Edmond," Peepers screamed. "We've got to get rid of that trailer," she said. "It's slowing us down too much. Just climb down there, Edmond. You can do it. Cats are good climbers."

"I can't," Edmond said fearfully.

"Scaredy cat!" Peepers replied calmly. "I'll do it myself."

Prodded by Peepers, Edmond reluctantly agreed to help and Patou took over at the steering wheel. Peepers and Edmond, who was now petrified with fear, crawled to the back of the Cadillac and tried to unhitch the trailer. But before they could loosen the hitch, the car hit a bump in the road. Peepers was bounced into the air while Edmond clung to the Cadillac's bumper.

"Help," cried Peepers as she clutched the chain connecting the Cadillac and the trailer's bumper.

"Hold on!" Edmond shouted.

Hunch took his knife and punctured one of the trailer's tires. Air hissed out of the flat tire and the trailer leaned dangerously to one side. The chain pulling the trailer suddenly snapped, tossing Peepers onto the vehicle's bumper. The trailer spun around out of control, then crashed into a wall near the Colonel's helicopter pad.

"Peepers! No!" Edmond screamed, his eyes wide with fear. He felt dizzy and disoriented and his imagination was running wild. He could see the Duke's evil face and hear his cruel laughter. Images of Colonel Pinky and his gang of goons flooded his brain. "Scaredy cat, scaredy cat," another voice inside his head said. Edmond thought about his new friends and his family back on the farm and how everyone was depending on him. Suddenly he knew he had to find the courage to act.

Edmond climbed back into the car and grabbed the steering wheel. "Guys, we're going back to get Peepers." He made a U-turn, the Cadillac's tires squealing. The Colonel's motorcycle-riding goons swerved sharply to avoid the oncoming Cadillac, then skidded and crashed.

Directly in the path of the Cadillac were the Colonel and Murray in the pink studio cart. Edmond drove towards them, picking up speed, going faster and faster.

"So, they want to play chicken," the Colonel noted with scorn.

"Don't worry," Murray said calmly. "I won't move."

"You idiot!" the Colonel shouted. "That's my car they're in."

At the last moment, the Colonel and Murray leapt out of the cart and the Cadillac bulldozed it out of the way. Snipes let go of the gas pedal and jumped on the brake pedal and the car skidded to a stop near a tall water tower. Edmond and his friends jumped out of the car and saw more goons coming their way. The only way out was up the rusting water tower ladder. Edmond, Goldie, and Patou, with the still-unconscious King slumped over his back, quickly scrambled up the ladder.

Colonel Pinky snapped at his goons, "Get up there and get them!"

Goldie wasn't watching where she was going and her foot slipped off the rungs of the ladder. She fell, but grabbed onto The King's leg. That put a terrible weight on Patou, who was clinging desperately to the edge of a platform near the top of the tower. Edmond grabbed Patou's paws and held them as tightly as he could, but the dog was too heavy. He could feel Patou losing his grip.

Snipes flew around the water tower sizing up the situation with his usual optimism. "We're all dead. We're all dead," he repeated.

Suddenly there was the groan of bending steel. All the weight from Patou, The King, and the Colonel's goons was putting an enormous strain on the tower supports. The girders began to buckle and the tower started falling.

"This is it," Patou yelled. "We're going down." He lost his grip and the animals plunged off the tower and tumbled through the air. All of a sudden, there was a roar of rotor blades as the Colonel's helicopter zoomed underneath the falling tower. In an amazing maneuver, the copter turned sideways and caught the animals in the open cargo bay doors. It soared skyward just as the water tower toppled to the ground with a deafening crash.

On the ground Colonel Pinky shouted, "What a catch, Murray." He picked up his radio and shouted into it, "Bring them in, Murray." There was no answer. "Murray?" he yelled. Still there was no answer. Then the Colonel noticed that Murray was standing next to him. The Colonel did a double take. Who could be flying the helicopter?

It was Peepers. After the trailer had crashed, she had climbed into the helicopter and started its engines. Now she was confidently handling the controls.

"I wonder who Murray is?" she said as her radio crackled with the Colonel's orders. "Let's see," Peepers said, "this is a Sikorsky X-62. These things are crazy."

Still, she managed to steer the helicopter up and away. In a few moments, the animals were leaving the city behind and heading back to the farm.

CHAPTER 7

In the flooded farmhouse Stuey was growing nervous. The flashlight was flickering on and off. "Oh, no!" he whined.

"Oh, yes. Oh, yes," the Duke replied in a cruel, mocking voice as he stuck his head in through the hole in the roof. He was growing hungry.

He turned to his fellow owls and said with a smile, "Gentlemen, go down and invite our friends to dinner. To be our dinner, that is."

The flashlight batteries died and the owls swooped down onto the barnyard animals. They tried to escape but the owls were too fast. Grabbing Stuey with their claws, they shoved an apple in his mouth.

"A picnic is so nice," the owls said happily. "We're so pleased you could join us for a meal." The owls broke out tablecloths, candles, and napkins.

"Now is the time to say your prayers," the Duke said to the animals. A second later he screamed, "Time's up. Pass the pork."

The owls pushed a captive Stuey down the table.

"Pass the pig," they said merrily. The Duke's mouth watered and he opened his beak wide to take a bite.

The room suddenly filled with the sound of whirling helicopter blades. A blinding beam from the copter's spotlight shot through the hole in the roof as the helicopter hovered above the farmhouse. The owls screamed in terror and their wings flapped frantically as they tried to escape the light.

Edmond grabbed the mouthpiece for the helicopter's communication system and turned on the loudspeakers.

"All right, you owls," his voice boomed. "This is Edmond. It's all over for you. We've got Chanticleer!"

When the farm animals heard this news, they cheered wildly. They were saved, but Edmond was still worried. "Where are my Mom and Dad and my brothers?" he asked. "I can't see them anywhere."

"Don't worry. We'll find them," Patou said reassuringly.

Edmond turned around and looked at Chanticleer's still-unconscious body. "How is Chanticleer, Goldie?" he asked.

She rubbed Chanticleer's head gently and he seemed to respond slightly to her touch. Then he opened one eye a little.

"I think he's waking up," Goldie exclaimed.

"Good, let's go in for a landing," Edmond replied.

As the helicopter descended, Hunch appeared. He had somehow flown into the copter and had been hiding in an air duct. He burst out and flew in for the kill.

"Annihilation," he cried triumphantly.

As he neared the cockpit, one of his legs became entangled in a strap on the wall of the helicopter. He tumbled through the air, landing on a fire extinguisher nearby. The impact made the extinguisher go off, and the blast of chemicals sent it, along with Hunch, rocketing around the helicopter cabin. Swirls of spray filled the cockpit as the extinguisher whizzed over the animals' heads. Hunch created such havoc that Peepers lost control of the helicopter. It began to fall rapidly and was spinning out of control.

"She's going down! Abandon ship," Peepers shouted.

The copter tumbled and then sank into the flood waters. The Duke watched the crash and he laughed with fiendish delight. "That takes care of the rooster," he thought happily.

Rain continued falling and the barnyard animals waited anxiously for the sound of Chanticleer's song. But it didn't come.

Chanticleer and the others had survived the crash. They were all a bit dazed, and Chanticleer was still groggy from the whack on the head he had gotten earlier. Goldie pulled Chanticleer out of the half-sunken helicopter and onto a large rock that stood nearby.

Chanticleer had no idea where he was. "Is it time for the show?" he muttered. "Where am I? Show me to the stage. Where's the microphone?" he asked.

"Chanti," Patou shouted in his ear. "You're home."

"Oh, my head," Chanticleer moaned. "It feels like I've been hit by an 800-pound mule. What happened?"

"There's no time to explain right now," Peepers snapped.

"Chanticleer, you've got to crow and you've got to crow now!" Patou demanded.

"The owls will be here any second," Edmond warned.

"Who are you?" Chanticleer asked, looking at the kitten.

"A friend," answered Peepers.

"Crow, Chanticleer. You've got to bring the sun back!" Peepers pleaded.

"I don't know if I can. I don't even know if I ever did," Chanticleer said sadly.

"Of course you did," Peepers stated emphatically.

"We were wrong," Patou said apologetically.

"It's your job to bring up the sun," Edmond insisted.

54

"It hasn't shined since you left," Peepers added.

"Look," said Chanticleer. He puffed up his chest once and then again. Nothing happened. He tried once more and out came a weak "Cock-a doo . . ." and nothing more.

"Cock-a-doo . . ." Chanticleer wheezed feebly. Gasping for air, the rooster collapsed.

"It's no use," Chanticleer moaned. "All I do is sing the blues now. Some King I am," he said with disgust.

"We don't want The King. We want Chanticleer," Edmond insisted.

There was a sudden fluttering of wings and there above them swarmed the Duke and his evil owls.

Patou growled menacingly and started to move toward the Duke. The Duke, however, used his powers to make Patou's loose shoelaces swirl around his feet, tying him up and immobilizing him.

"I know it's frightfully impolite to eavesdrop like this, but are you having trouble with your throat, Chanticleer? Nothing to say?" the Duke mocked. "Cock-a-doodle-doo, perhaps." He moved towards Chanticleer with hate in his eyes.

Chanticleer couldn't speak, much less sing. The Duke summoned his strength and picked up Chanticleer and tossed him into the mud. The Duke then pounded Chanticleer chest-deep into the soft ground.

"Come on, Chanticleer. Crow!" Edmond cried.

Turning to the rest of the animals, he said, "Let's show him we believe. Say his name and he'll get his power back. Come on, Chanticleer! Chanticleer! Chanticleer!"

"Silence," thundered the Duke. The Duke suddenly seemed to be growing larger and larger. His body seemed to be surging with power. The Duke created two shafts of crackling energy that surrounded Edmond and wrapped themselves around his neck.

"Leave him alone," Chanticleer shouted. "It's me you want." But the Duke ignored him.

Edmond gasped for air as the Duke used his power to raise him off the ground and high into the air. The Duke's power shot through Edmond's body, engulfing it with crackling current. Then suddenly the force subsided and the kitten fell to the ground, his body totally limp and seemingly lifeless. The animals were petrified and they fell silent.

"You stupid nincompoops," the Duke said, sneering. "You really thought you could defeat me?"

While the Duke had been busy with Edmond, Peepers had freed Patou. The dog crept over Edmond's body and gently nuzzled his cheek. Patou angrily whispered Chanticleer's name. Then he said it a little louder. "Chanticleer." Defiantly, he began chanting, "Chanticleer. Chanticleer.

Chanticleer." Each time he said the name louder and louder.

"Very stupid, Patou," the Duke said scornfully.

Peepers joined in the chant. Then Snipes and Goldie began chanting Chanticleer's name, too. Soon all the animals joined in.

The Duke's chest swelled with rage. Some of his fellow owls were growing nervous. The Duke was losing control over the situation as more and more animals chanted Chanticleer's name.

Chanticleer knew he had to help his friends now or it would all be over. He drew in a deep breath and tried to crow. But only a tiny little cackle came out. The Duke turned on the chanting animals with fury in his voice.

"Fools! All of you. Silence!" The Duke let his words sink in. "You want Chanticleer? I'll give you Chanticleer," he shouted. Then the Duke began to spin. As he did, he grew larger and larger until he stood taller than the farmhouse. Soon he grew taller than the tallest tree in the forest. The Duke spun faster and faster, creating a giant tornado. The force was so great that tree branches, floating barrels and boxes, and even a bed were swept up into the mighty tornado.

Memories of the happy days on the farm began flooding Chanticleer's brain. If he were ever going to save the farm and his friends, he knew that time had to be now. It was his last chance.

He summoned all his strength and drew in a deep, deep breath. "Cock-a-doodle-doo," he roared. It was a magnificent crow, a song that echoed through the sky, filling the valleys and reaching the highest mountain peaks. It traveled through the upper reaches of the atmosphere and resounded through the heavens, reaching the stars themselves.

The song was still echoing through the sky when a tiny sliver of light appeared on the horizon. It grew and grew until a shaft of sunlight peeked through a break in the dark clouds. Breaks in the clouds began to appear and the sun began to rise and pierce the gloom. The Duke—still spinning and still creating dark storm clouds—reached out to try and attack Chanticleer, but at that very moment, a dazzling ray of sunlight shot over the hillside. It was like a bolt of lightning and it struck the Duke directly. His spinning began to slow and then it ceased. He began spinning in the opposite direction. The animals shuddered as they heard the Duke scream in pain.

The sun continued to rise, spreading golden light all over the farm. Soon, the storm clouds that had surrounded the Duke evaporated and disappeared. When they did, all that was left was a tiny, shrunken Duke, who was now no bigger than a mouse. One of the barnyard mice approached the little owl, but the Duke was terrified now that he was tiny. He tried to jump into the water to escape, but he landed right in the arms of Hunch, who was now five times his size. Hunch picked up the little creature and laughed.

"It's me, Uncle Dukey," the Duke said in a high squeaky voice.

"Dukey?" Hunch asked. "Come here, Dukey. Ho ho ho."

Hunch grabbed his knife and flicked the switch. Out popped a large flyswatter. It was just the blade Hunch wanted. The Duke flapped his wings frantically trying to escape.

"Hunch, don't," the Duke begged. "Please . . ."

Hunch quickly gave him a smash with the swatter. "Animation. Annihilation," he said joyfully. "Oooh, that's music to my ears. Hold still, you little twerp," Hunch demanded. "Aggravation. Abomination. Alienation. Altercation. ANNIHILATION!" Hunch screamed.

Hunch chased the tiny Duke across the water and over the hills until they disappeared beyond the horizon.

As the sun burned through the last of the clouds, the rains stopped and the flood began to subside. The animals were happy at first, but then they realized that Edmond still lay lifeless before them. They gathered solemnly around his body. They had no idea how to help him or even if they could.

"He was so brave," Peepers said, crying.

Just then a beam of shimmering sunlight streaked down through the sky, landing on Edmond and bathing his body in warm, brilliant light. Edmond's body began to glow and so did the ground beneath him. The animals gasped in amazement as Edmond's body began to change. His body grew larger and the fur began to disappear. Slowly he was transformed into a boy with curly blond hair and rosy cheeks. The ground he had been lying on became a bed.

"He *was* a boy," Snipes said in amazement.

"Oh, he was such a handsome boy," Peepers said sadly, as Edmond still lay there lifeless. "Oh, Edmond. Edmond . . . Edmond . . ."

CHAPTER 8

"Edmond. Edmond. Edmond," a gentle voice called out.

Edmond heard his name being called. His head hurt but his brow felt cool and moist.

"Edmond honey, wake up." It was his mother. "Come on now, please. Wake up, Edmond."

Edmond opened his eyes. It was his mother and she was wiping a cool washcloth across his forehead. Edmond sat up, wiped the sleep from his eyes, and said, "Mom . . . Mom . . . it's you, and . . ." Then he noticed his hands.

"Look," he exclaimed. "I'm not furry anymore. I'm a boy. Mom, I'm a boy!" Edmond couldn't contain himself.

"Yes you are, and you've got a nasty bump on your head. Lie down now," she said gently.

"The Duke turned me into a cat and was going to eat me, but Patou bit him on the leg . . ." Edmond exclaimed.

Then Edmond noticed a thin shaft of sunlight peeking through his window. The window was covered with a blanket, but a few rays of sunshine were coming through. Edmond ran to the window and pulled the blanket aside. He looked outside and saw his father and brothers cleaning up some of the debris the flood had left. It was a beautiful day with sunlight streaming across the yard. The cow that had been trapped in the mud was now happily munching grass in the yard. The flood waters had already begun to dry up.

Edmond's father looked up and saw him in the window. A big smile appeared on his face and he called out to his son.

"How are you, Edmond?"

"Fine. But where is Chanticleer and the gang?" Edmond turned to his mother and said, "Chanticleer raised the sun."

"Chanticleer is just a storybook character," his mother replied. "He's only make-believe. Now you go back to bed."

"No, Mom, I saw them . . . Patou, Peepers, Snipes, Chanti, Stuey . . . I saw them all. I never got to say goodbye to them. They're probably wondering what happened to me. They probably think I'm dead. I've got to tell them I'm okay."

"They know, honey," his mother said gently.

"Think so?" Edmond asked.

"Yes," she said with certainty.

Edmond felt a cool breeze on his face and took a deep breath of the spring air. Suddenly his head didn't hurt anymore.

Edmond's mother guided him gently back to bed

and said, "Now I want you to rest for a little while. If you need anything, I'll be downstairs. Just holler."

As his mother left the room, Edmond picked up his storybook and stared at the cover.

"Welcome home, Chanti," he said softly. "Thanks for bringing back the sun."

Just then, a rooster crowed with a powerful "Cock-a-doodle-doo." It was as if Chanticleer had heard him and had sung a song just for him.

Edmond suddenly felt very happy. He rushed back to his window and stuck his head out. The morning sun felt wonderfully warm on his face. Birds were chirping and insects were buzzing and Edmond could swear he heard music in the air. Edmond couldn't wait to get outside and play. There was no doubt about it. It was going to be a great day!